To my parents and older brother,
and also my grandpa, whom I shall miss for ever
Y. L.-Q.

FEBRUARY
9
2013
除夕

First published 2008 by Hsin Yi Publications, Taipei, Taiwan

This edition published 2012 by Walker Books Ltd
87 Vauxhall Walk, London SE11 5HJ
by arrangement with Hsin Yi Publications

2 4 6 8 10 9 7 5 3 1

Text © 2007 Yu Li-Qiong
Illustrations © 2007 Zhu Cheng-Liang

The right of Yu Li-Qiong and Zhu Cheng-Liang
to be identified as author and illustrator respectively
of this work has been asserted by them in accordance
with the Copyright, Designs and Patents Act 1988

This book has been typeset in Myriad Tilt

Printed in China

British Library Cataloguing in Publication Data: a catalogue record
for this book is available from the British Library

ISBN 978-1-4063-3857-7
www.walker.co.uk

A NEW YEAR'S
REUNION

Yu Li-Qiong

Illustrated by Zhu Cheng-Liang

WALKER BOOKS
AND SUBSIDIARIES
LONDON · BOSTON · SYDNEY · AUCKLAND

Daddy builds big houses in faraway places.
He comes home only once each year,
during Chinese New Year.

Today, Mummy and I wake up really early because ...

Daddy is coming home.

I watch him from a distance, not daring to get close.
Daddy comes over and sweeps me up in his arms,
prickling my face with his beard.
"Mummy!" I cry in alarm.

"Look what I've got for you!" Daddy rummages in
his big suitcase and takes out — ooh, what a pretty hat!
Mummy has a new padded coat, too.

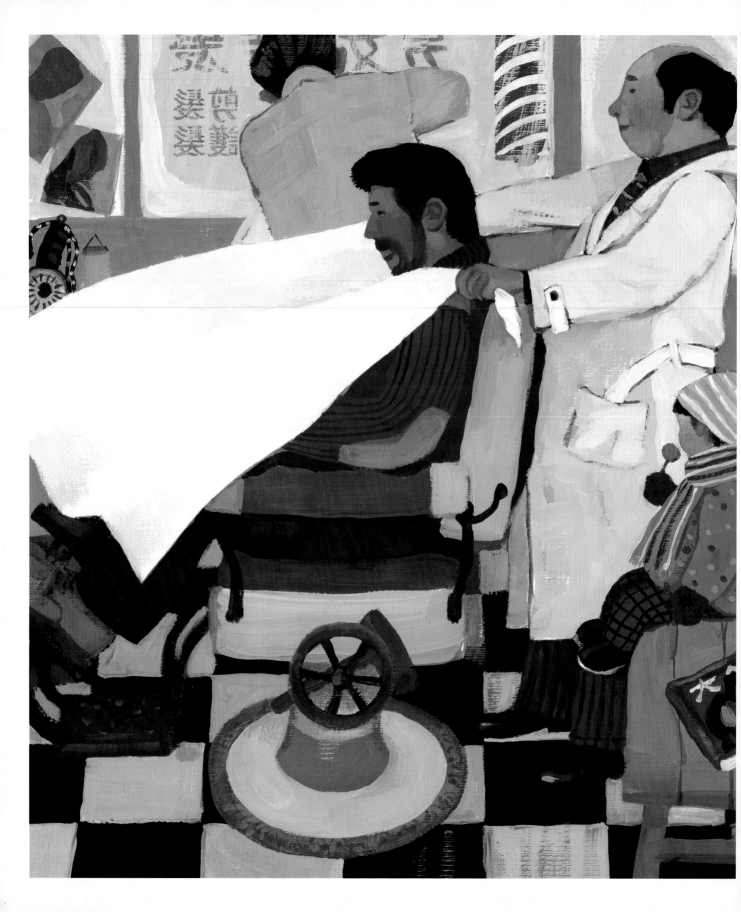

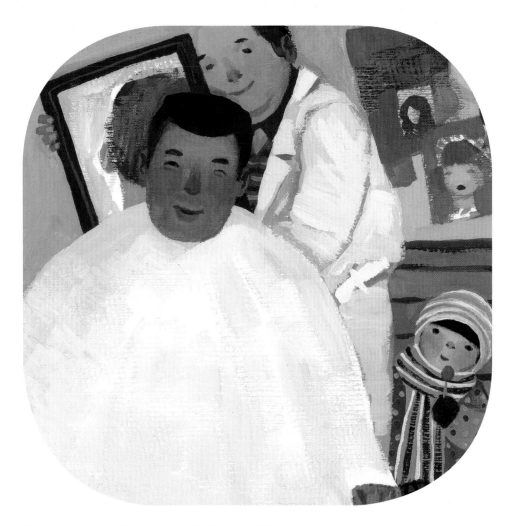

"Let's go and have a haircut. Then everything will go
smoothly in the coming year," Daddy says to me after lunch.
I sit on a chair, waiting.

The Daddy in the mirror is getting more like
Daddy the way he used to be.

Later, it's time to make sticky rice balls. Daddy buries a coin in one of the balls and says, "Whoever finds the ball with the coin will have good luck."

Pop, pop, pop, bang, bang, bang!

We hear firecrackers outside all night.
I lie between Daddy and Mummy and fall asleep,
drowsily hearing them whispering, whispering…

Early the next morning, Mummy serves up piping-hot
sticky rice balls, and Daddy feeds them to me with a spoon.
Suddenly, I bite on something hard. "The fortune coin!
It's the fortune coin!" I shout.
"Good for you, Maomao! Quick, put it away in your pocket so
the good luck won't escape!" Daddy is more excited than I am.

Mummy helps me into a brand-new jacket –
we're going New Year visiting!

On the way, I meet my friend Dachun.

"Maomao, where are you going?"

"I'm out for New Year visits with my daddy!"

"Me too. Look, I got a big red envelope!"

"Well, how about this..." I take the coin out
of my pocket. "I have a fortune coin! My daddy
buried it in a sticky rice ball and I found it!"

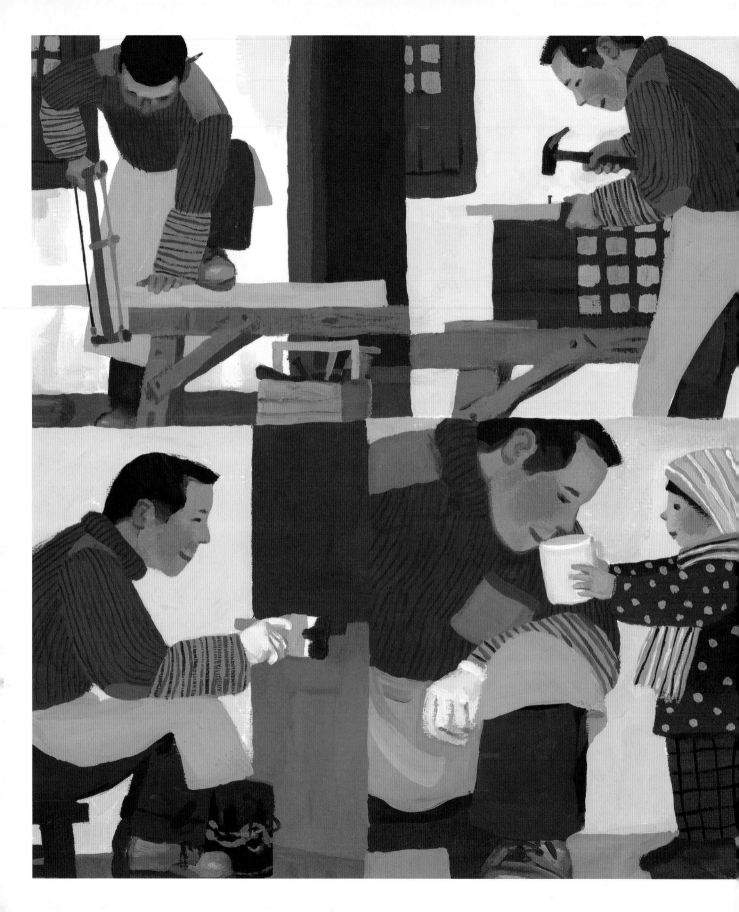

On the second day of New Year, the sky is gloomy,
and it looks as if it's going to snow. Daddy gets busy
fixing the windows, painting the door
and changing the light bulbs —
and the whole house brightens up.

"Come on, let's fix the roof!" Daddy winks.
Excellent! Mummy never allows me up there alone!

Hey, I can see Dachun's roof!

"Listen, what's that sound over there?" I say.

"Oh, it's the dragon dance in the main street." Daddy
straightens up and looks into the distance.

"Where is it? Where is it?" I stand on tiptoe,
stretching up as far as I can.

Daddy puts me on his shoulders. "Now can you see it?" he asks.

"Yes, I can. They're coming!"

On the third day of New Year, it snows — really hard!

When it finally stops, Dachun and the other children come and get me to go and play. We build a huge snowman in the courtyard and have a snowball fight.

I don't go home till it's getting dark.

I feel inside my pocket and ... I can't find the coin!

My fortune coin is gone!

I rush out to the courtyard, but it's all covered
in snow. Where is my fortune coin?

"Don't cry, sweetie. I'll give you another one.
Look, it's exactly the same!" Daddy scoops another
coin out of his pocket.
"I don't want that one – I want the other one!" I bawl.

In the evening, I creep into bed, miserable, but as I take
off my jacket, **clink!** – something falls on the floor.
It's the coin! My fortune coin!
"Daddy, come quick – come and see! I haven't lost
the fortune coin. It's been with me all the time."

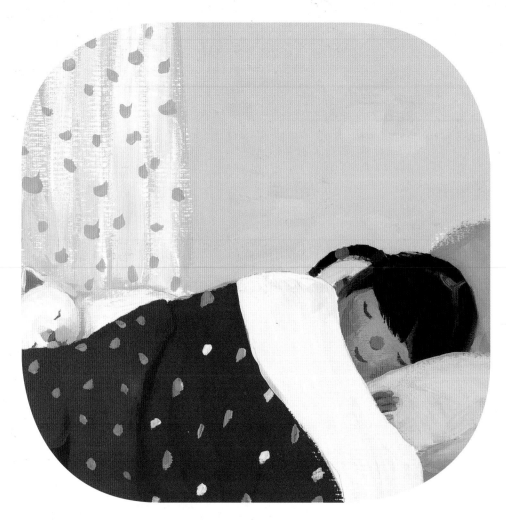

That night, I sleep very soundly.

When I get up the next morning,
I see Mummy helping Daddy pack.
Daddy is leaving today.

Soon, Daddy's packing is done. He crouches down
and gives me a big hug, whispering in my ear,
"Next time Daddy's back, he'll give you a doll, OK?"

"No." I shake my head hard and say,
"I want to give **you** something..."

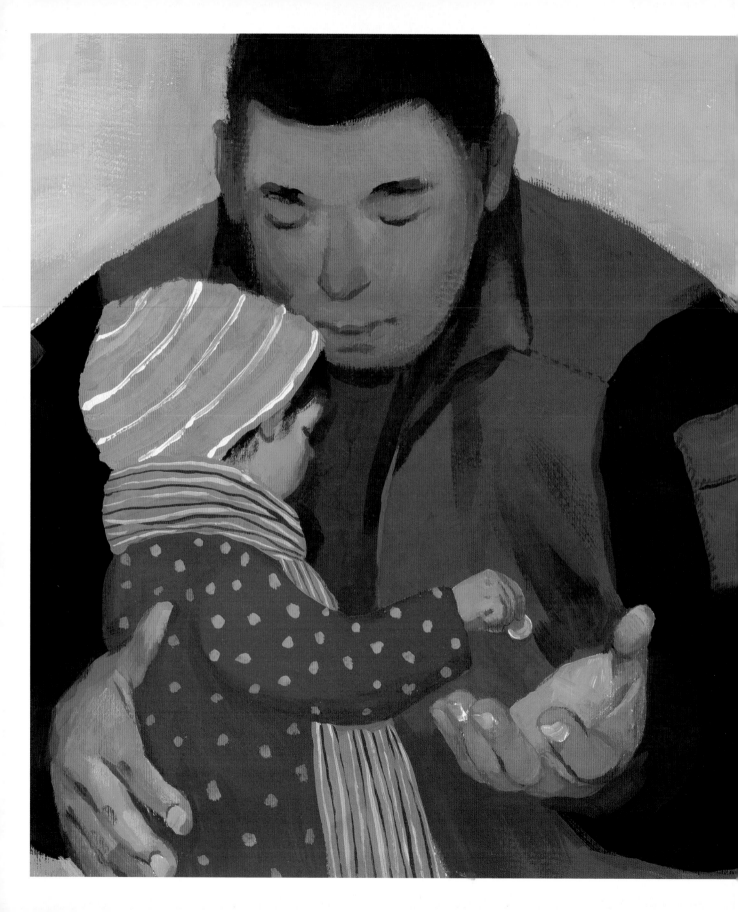

I put the coin, all warm from being held
in my hand for so long, in Daddy's palm and say,
"Here, take this. Next time you're back, we can
bury it in the sticky rice ball again!"

Daddy is very quiet.
He nods, and hugs me tight.

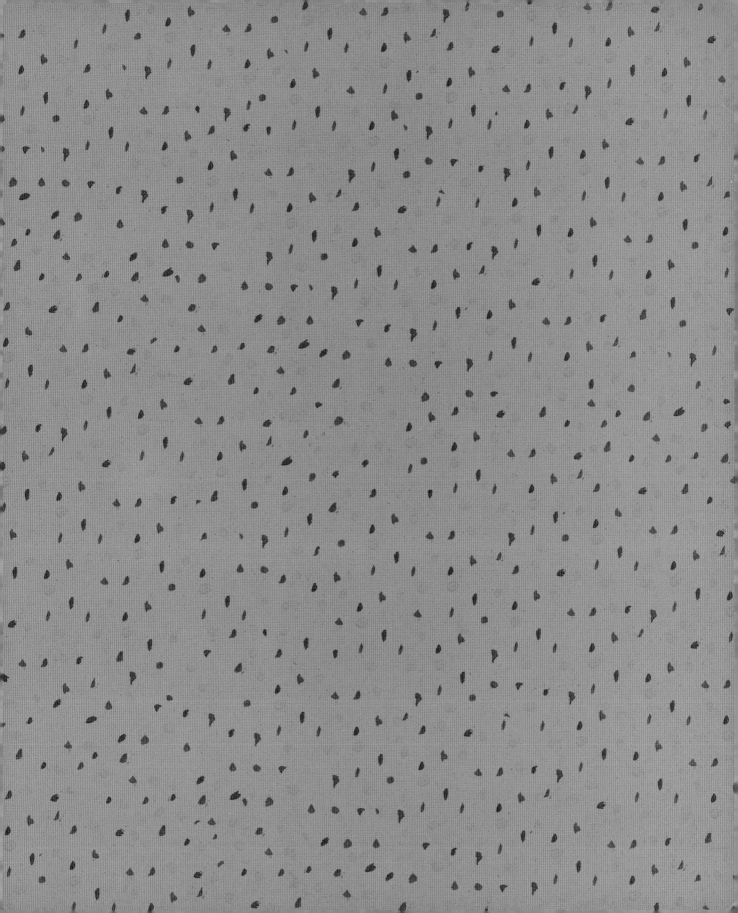

The family in this book is a fictional one, but there are in reality over 100 million migrant workers in China, many of whom work hundreds or sometimes thousands of miles away from home, returning only once each year, for just a few days, at New Year.

Author **Yu Li-Qiong** was born in Anqing in the People's Republic of China in 1980. She gained a BA in literature from Nanjing University and subsequently an MA in dramatic art. A member of the Chinese Institute of Prose and currently editor of **Eastern Dolls**, she has published more than a hundred thousand words of writing in prose and novels since 1996. She lives in Nanjing.

Illustrator **Zhu Cheng-Liang** was born in Shanghai in 1948. He graduated from the Fine Arts Department of Nanjing Art School and is currently deputy chief editor at the Jiangsu Fine Arts Publishing House. His achievements include an Honourable Mention by UNESCO's Noma Concours for Picture Book Illustrations, for his children's book **Flashing Rabbit-Shaped Lamp**. He too lives in Nanjing.